THE CASE OF
The Disappearing Detective

A SHERLOCK HOLMES
EASTER MYSTERY

by

J. Lawrence Matthews

ISBN: 978-1-7366783-9-8 (Paperback)
ISBN: 979-8-9993178-0-3 (eBook)

Library of Congress Control Number: 2025923094

Any references to historical events, real people, or real places are used fictitiously. All characters, incidents, and dialogue are drawn from the author's imagination and are not to be construed as real.

East Dean Press
Naples, FL

"What is the meaning of it, Watson?" said Holmes solemnly as he laid down the paper.

"What object is served by this circle of misery and violence and fear? It must tend to some end, or else our universe is ruled by chance, which is unthinkable. But what end? There is the great standing perennial problem to which human reason is as far from an answer as ever."

| **The Adventure of the Cardboard Box**
  by Sir Arthur Conan Doyle

A Caller at the Door

It was the morning of Good Friday 1903, and I was seated at the breakfast table reading an account of the King's impending state visit to Paris when there came a tremendous ring at the bell. I was annoyed, for my surgery wouldn't open for another hour, and our servant girl was in the kitchen and couldn't hear the bell, so I waited for the caller to give up.

But the ringing persisted, and finally I set down the *Times*, rose from the table, and answered the door.

To my great surprise, the unwelcome caller turned out to be very welcome indeed. It was none other than Mrs. Hudson, Sherlock Holmes's landlady.

"It's Mr. Holmes," she said without preamble. "He's

been away on a case for two days and hasn't returned. Hasn't telegraphed. Hasn't *anything*."

"That's hardly unusual," said I, inviting her inside.

"But I'm to leave by the morning express for family in the North, and he had assured me he would return in time to escort me to the station."

"Then he'll be back," said I, soothingly. "Come in. A cup of tea would—"

"Thank you, Doctor, but this is not like him. Mr. Holmes always keeps me informed when he is detained on a case. Why, he was stranded in the Shetlands last Michaelmas but still got a message through to Baker Street!"

"Where has he gone this time? The Continent?"

She shook her head. "East Dean, in the South Downs."

"I've never heard of it."

"It's a small village outside of Eastbourne. He was there once on a case and rather liked it." She wrung her hands. "This Wednesday evening a gentleman called about some bad business in the area, and next thing I knew Mr. Holmes was catching the train to Eastbourne. I believe he is planning to visit an estate agent there as well."

"An estate agent! He is *moving*?"

"I can't say—I don't know. Please, Doctor." She pointed at the hall clock. "The express leaves in an hour and I am at my wit's end whether to stay or go. Mr. Holmes should have contacted me by now."

"Perhaps the telegraph lines are down? The weather has been harsh—"

"The lines are up," she said impatiently. "I inquired at the district office."

My wife now appeared on the stairs. She could see at once that something was troubling our old friend.

"John! Why do you leave Mrs. Hudson standing outside? Take her coat! Offer tea!"

"I did, but—"

"Thank you, Mrs. Watson. But I haven't come to call on you. It's Mr. Holmes…."

And with that, the story of the disappearing detective tumbled forth from Mrs. Hudson's lips once more. When she had finished, my wife stared at me, her eyebrows arched.

"What?" I exclaimed, "I've invited her to come in three times!"

"It isn't that, John," she said severely. "The question is, why are you still here?"

AN HOUR LATER I WAS at Victoria Station, in an express bound for Eastbourne. I placed my umbrella, valise, and medical kit—which I had brought just in case it was needed—on the rack and took my seat. Then, as the carriage moved slowly out of the station, I opened the morning edition of the *Eastbourne Chronicle* which I had purchased at the station and began reading the criminal news.

I was looking for whatever might have drawn Sherlock Holmes to the South Downs.

There were the usual accounts of petty horse thefts and house break-ins, of course, but more promising was the report of a recent spate of vandalism at the new lighthouse going up at Beachy Head, between Eastbourne and East Dean.

It seems lamp-oil had been dumped on the granite blocks, making them dangerous to lift into place, and a local species of poisonous jellyfish had been found in the carpenter's shed, scaring off the men.

But the police had put it all down to lads from the Eastbourne estates "having a laugh," and so, seeing nothing else that might have required my friend's great powers of deduction, I set the paper aside and let the gentle rocking of the carriage lull me to sleep.

I awoke as we were pulling into the Eastbourne station, where I found a hansom cab to take me to East Dean. After a half-hour ride up the coast road in a driving rain, I was deposited on a corner of the village green outside the Tiger Inn, just as the rain stopped.

The Tiger is an ancient pub, its low ceilings held up by thick oak beams, and it proved a most welcome sanctuary, with a fire roaring in the grate, a noisy

game of darts going in the snug and a friendly-looking landlord behind the taps.

Yes, he said, lunch was being served (he recommended the fish and chips), and certainly, he did have a spare room for the night (although he warned I might find it a bit noisy until they stopped serving dinner at nine o'clock).

When I asked if a man from London had recently taken a room there, however, he ignored my question, turned his attention to the counter—which looked clean enough already—and began wiping it with a cloth.

"Now, see here, my good man. This fellow is a friend of mine, and I'm worried." I spoke quietly, avoiding the use of Sherlock Holmes's name in such a public place. "He came down from London Wednesday evening and hasn't been heard from since. I'm here to find him."

The landlord stopped and met my gaze.

"And how did you say you know him?"

"We worked together for many years."

"And your name is?"

"Watson. John H. Watson." I lifted my medical kit and showed him the stenciled name on the black leather. A broad smile crossed his face, and he put down his rag.

"The genuine article! Delighted to meet you. Name's Jack." He glanced around the pub, busy with a lunchtime crowd. "We try to give Mr. *Gibson* his privacy, you see."

That Holmes was calling himself 'Gibson' did not surprise me in the least. He sometimes used an alias when his work took him to small villages such as this, for my stories had made him famous even in the most unlikely of places, and he preferred to conduct his inquiries undisturbed.

"I understand completely. Can you tell me where I might find him?"

The landlord shook his head. "Never tells me

anything, guv. Bit of a lone wolf, you know. Always takes the room out back over the stables. Comes and goes as he pleases."

"So, he's been here before?"

"Couple of times over the years."

"Any idea what brought him this time?" I asked.

"Well, I expect it had to do with that business out at Beachy Head."

"But the police said it was lads from the estates having a laugh."

"That's no job to be having a laugh with, guv. Men get hurt when those blocks fall on 'em!"

"Well, when did you last see 'Mr. Gibson?'"

"Yesterday. There." He nodded at one of the tables. "He was having breakfast with old Ingalls."

"Old who?"

"Ingalls. George Ingalls. Runs the telegraph station out at Birling Gap, where the lines come in from France."

The mystery deepened: Holmes had met with the telegraph operator, yet he had sent no telegram to Mrs. Hudson!

"Do you know what they were discussing?"

"Property, I expect. Ingalls also looks after the parish land records for the council. Has time on his hands, you see. His wife died a few years back. I got the impression he was showing your friend some papers about a cottage in the area."

"Did you happen to overhear where it is?"

"No, and they didn't talk about it long." Jack leaned in. "Ingalls recognized 'Mr. Gibson' from your books— got so excited he jumped up and banged his head on a beam! I had to get him a sticking plaster. Then he started asking your friend questions." He touched the side of his nose. "Calls himself a 'Sherlockian,' you see."

"Ah." I *did* see.

I have never mentioned them before, but some of my readers develop a kind of obsession with Sherlock

Holmes. A few even formed a 'society' here in London devoted to my stories, going so far as to take the names of the characters for their own! We encountered them occasionally over the years, Holmes and I, lingering outside 221B at all hours, hoping for a glimpse or an autograph.

But never in the countryside.

"Did they leave here together?"

"No. Ingalls went runnin' off to the church, head still bleedin', probably to get more papers. Your friend wrapped up his fish and chips in a newspaper—he couldn't eat for all the questions—and went off somewhere with his walking stick."

"Where will I find this Ingalls now?"

"Telegraph station." The landlord waved his rag at the door. "Out the pub, across the green, you'll find yourself on Went Way. Follow it to the last house—that's old widow Dunbar's place, she died last year—and you'll come to a footpath just after. Take the footpath a mile or so across the Downs. Make straight for the old lighthouse, Belle Tout, can't miss her. Sits up on the bluff—"

"That's the one being replaced by the lighthouse going up at Beachy Head?"

"Right. Head straight for Belle Tout, but just before you get there, you'll see the telegraph house to your right, down on the beach at Birling Gap. Ingalls should be in there, beavering away."

"Thank you, Jack."

"Not at all."

"One more thing. Does anyone else in the village know who 'Mr. Gibson' really is?"

"Only a few of us. We try to leave him alone. He's a good man, your friend."

"Thank you—and if you see him, please tell him I'm looking for him."

"Will do, guv."

I departed the Tiger and crossed the green as

instructed. Upon reaching Went Way, however, I spotted a butcher's window next to the old bakehouse, and I recalled something Holmes had once told me.

Whenever he travelled to a new village on a case, he said, he stopped in at the local butcher's.

"After all, Watson, the butcher knows *everyone* in a small village."

And East Dean was a very small village.

"GOOD MORNING."

"Morning, sir." The butcher wore a straw hat and a white apron stained with blood, and he was cutting sausage links from a long tube of encased meat and slapping them atop a growing pile on the scale, his eyes fixed upon the needle. "How can I help?"

After my experience with Jack at the Tiger, I decided

the direct way was the best, so instead of asking discreetly about Sherlock Holmes, I simply lifted my medical kit onto the counter and pointed to my name.

He took one glance, put down the links, wiped his hands on the filthy apron, and shook mine with enthusiasm. "I'll be. Dr. Watson! Honored to have you in our village, sir!"

"Thank you." I shook his sticky palm somewhat ruefully, and he offered me a wet towel.

"Sorry! Forget myself sometimes. Looking for 'Mr. Gibson,' are you?"

"Yes, I take it he's been here?"

The butcher nodded. "Came 'round yesterday morning asking about that business at Beachy Head. Then he rushed right out and I haven't seen him since."

This was progress, anyway: Holmes *had* come to East Dean to investigate the lighthouse vandals.

"Any idea where he might be now?"

"Find George Ingalls. I hear they had a natter

yesterday at the Tiger."

"Yes, Jack told me. What does he look like, this Ingalls?"

"Oh, average fellow, but he wears thick black spectacles. And one of those hats." He slapped the last of the sausages onto the pile and began wrapping the mass in wax paper.

"What kind of hat?"

"You know. The Sherlock Holmes hat." Now he tied up the bundle with string. "'Deerstalker,' he calls it."

I had never heard of such a thing, but I let it go. Sherlockians had some funny ideas, I knew.

"He'll be at the telegraph station now?"

"Expect so. If he's not at the lighthouse helping Otto."

"Otto?"

"The Belle Tout lightkeeper. Well, not for long. Poor old sod's getting the sack when the new one goes up at Beachy Head." He shook his head. "Gone a bit doolally since they started work on it, has Otto. Won't let anybody get near Belle Tout except Ingalls. Chased the postman off with a harpoon last week. Thought he was the bailiff, come to take him away—"

He looked up from his work, an odd expression upon his face.

"What is it?" I asked.

"This order. These bangers." He pointed to the scale.

"That's five pounds' worth of meat."

"What of it?"

"This is the second order from Otto in two days!"

"So?"

"It's only Otto there at the lighthouse, yeah?"

"I fail to see—"

"Who's eating all these sausages, then?" he asked, tapping the package with his forefinger.

A cold hand gripped me as the thought of Sherlock Holmes somehow being taken prisoner at the lighthouse sprang to mind.

I thanked the butcher and departed at once, umbrella in one hand, medical kit in the other.

And a heavy packet of sausages tucked inside my coat.

I Am Interrogated

So anxious was I to find my old friend that it was not until I reached the top of Went Hill and paused for breath that I realized how beautiful were the Sussex Downs and why Sherlock Holmes had become so attracted to the area he was considering a move there!

The trees atop the hillside stood hunched like tired washerwomen, bent low by the fierce winds off the Channel; in the swales were nestled stone cottages, their varied barns and outbuildings testifying to the specialty of each farmer who lived within; and in every pasture lurked the signs of their varied livelihoods: skittish sheep or placid cows or swarms of boisterous starlings pecking up seeds from newly planted fields.

It was lonely and quite desolate, but it was also quite entrancing.

And it was presided over by a grand sentinel standing barely one hundred yards from the great chalk cliffs overlooking the English Channel.

The Belle Tout lighthouse.

SEEN UP CLOSE, SHE CONSISTED of a granite tower perhaps one hundred feet high, with a two-story house attached rather like a barnacle to her landward side. I picked my way around the tower to a walled courtyard that protected the living quarters from passersby. This I entered through the unlocked gate and walked quietly past a henhouse, a rabbit hutch, and tall stacks of firewood to the unlit entryway.

A window above the door showed lights were on in

the upper floor, but no one keeping watch. As I wasn't certain what danger lurked within, my plan was to use the sausages as a kind of Trojan Horse.

"Bangers!" I yelled up at the window in a business-like voice, pounding my fist on the door. "I come from the butcher!" Receiving no response, I pounded once more. "Sausages! Butcher sent me!"

Suddenly, the face of a man appeared in the window above. He wore thick spectacles and an oddly shaped cloth hat.

George Ingalls, no doubt, in his "deerstalker."

He studied me carefully.

I held up the packet and motioned for him to come down.

He turned away briefly, then reappeared in the window. I was about to bang again when I heard the sliding of a bolt. Then the door before me opened a crack, and a pair of suspicious, watery eyes fixed upon me from beneath a shock of grey hair held down by a woolen sailor's cap.

The old lightkeeper, I presumed.

"Wha'd'ya want?" said he, in a gruff, suspicious voice.

"I bring sausages from the butcher."

"But you ain't the butcher!"

"I've come in his place."

"You the bailiff, then?"

"Bailiff? No, I'm a friend of Sherlock Holmes. Is he here?"

The suspicious eye blinked.

"He *is* here, isn't he?"

"Leave the bangers and go 'way!"

"I have come to see my friend and won't leave until I do. I am Dr. John H. Watson—"

"Don't care who y'are! Go 'way!" The door slammed shut.

"I will not go away. I've come for Sherlock Holmes." I could hear the heavy bolt being thrown. *I am Dr.*

John Watson! Open up!"

Stepping back, I saw the face had gone from the window. Soon I heard rapid footfalls clanging upon metallic stairs, followed by raised voices. I was about to put my shoulder to the door when the bolt was thrown back and a different face appeared.

The face from the window, eyes bulging behind thick spectacles and odd cap upon his head: George Ingalls.

"Are you really Dr. Watson? *The* Dr. Watson?" he asked breathlessly.

"Yes, of course. Why? Do you think I go around impersonating the man?"

"One can't be too careful! Come in, Doctor, come in!"

The door swung open, and I stepped inside a drafty, low-ceilinged basement smelling of paraffin and lit by a single oil lamp hanging from an overhead beam.

Beside the door, a fishing rod was leaned up against

the wall, and next to this, an old yellow mac hung on a peg. Beyond the mac was the source of the strong paraffin odor: three large casks of lamp-oil.

But my attention was quickly taken by the figure standing in the center of the basement at the bottom of a circular metal staircase.

It was the man who had first answered the door.

He was an ancient-looking mariner, and he eyed me distrustfully while holding what appeared to be a kind of shepherd's staff.

My heart almost stopped when I realized the staff was, in fact, an old harpoon.

"Mind the rafters," said Ingalls, slamming the door shut behind me and bolting it.

"What about him?" I asked.

"Oh, Otto? He's harmless." Ingalls removed his cap and waved it at the lightkeeper. "It's all right, Otto, you may stand down. He's only a doctor."

"Thank you," I said, as the lightkeeper stood at ease.

Relaxing my guard, I studied my surroundings in the dim light, and could make out piles of coiled rope, buoys, rescue flares, and life jackets. Also, an irregular

mass of flotsam evidently scavenged from the shore— the physical manifestations of a lightkeeper's lonely travels.

But no sign of Sherlock Holmes.

"Where is he?" I demanded. "Where is Sherlock Holmes?"

Ingalls appeared taken aback. "Why, he's upstairs,

sleeping! Didn't get much rest last night, is all." He had been studying me by the light of the oil-lamp, and I could see the wound where he had banged his head at the Tiger.

It was raw and ugly.

"You should have that looked at," I said, pointing to his forehead. "I'm a doctor, I could—"

"Never mind me!" Ingalls snapped, suddenly wary. "You don't *look* much like Dr. Watson."

"For goodness' sake, man. What should I look like?"

"Paget's drawings. From the stories."

I snorted. "Do you really think Mr. Paget draws us from life and not from his own fertile imagination?"

"Sherlock Holmes certainly looks like *his* drawings."

"Yes, and I want to see him!" I snapped.

He eyed me distrustfully. "First, answer my question, if you really are Dr. Watson."

"What do you mean 'if?'"

"Tell me, where, exactly, were you wounded?"

"I beg your pardon?"

His eyes grew large behind the thick lenses. "You served in Afghanistan, and you were wounded. *Where* were you wounded?"

"At the battle of Maiwand—"

"No, no. *Where on your body*? Leg or shoulder?"

He was growing agitated, so I answered soothingly, as Sherlock Holmes had always done when confronted by an unbalanced witness.

"I'm sorry, I don't understand your question—"

"*A Study in Scarlet*! Afghanistan!" he abruptly shouted. "The Jezail bullet that struck you on the shoulder. You write it '*shattered the bone and grazed the subclavian artery.*' Yet in *The Sign of the Four*—the very next book!—you nurse a wounded *leg*! Which is it, Doctor? Leg or shoulder? The *real* Dr. Watson would know!"

He spoke quickly, nervously, hands clasping and unclasping. I was taken aback by his passionate recitation of details from old stories so little remembered by me.

"It was both places, if you must know," I said with an effort at self-composure. "I took a bullet to my shoulder in the field and a second to the leg while my orderly was fixing me to a packhorse."

He snorted in disbelief. "How is it, then, that you profess yourself a fast runner?"

"A fast what?"

"*Hound of the Baskervilles*! Dartmoor! The pursuit of the deadly hound! '*Never have I seen a man run as Holmes ran that night,*' you write! '*I am reckoned fleet of foot, but he outpaced me.*'" Ingalls spoke the words as if from a sacred text, eyes blazing. "How could you be 'fleet of foot' if you'd taken a bullet to your leg in Afghanistan?"

Again, his agitation was severe, and again I tried to sooth him.

"Well, I suppose I exaggerated my physical

attributes somewhat, for the sake of the story. Does it really matter?"

"*Of course it matters!*" he shouted, glittery eyes popping. "A Sherlock Holmes story must *be rational!* *Precise!* Like Sherlock *Holmes!*"

My blood began to boil.

Who on earth did he think *wrote* those stories?

"Well, it wouldn't have been very exciting if I said, '*Thanks to smoking his wretched pipe all those years, Sherlock Holmes could barely outrun a fat doctor like me,*' would it?"

I held out the packet for him.

"Now see here, I've answered your questions, I'm obviously *the* Dr. Watson, so take these cursed sausages off my hands and lead me to Sherlock Holmes!"

He seemed on the verge of another outburst when a very familiar, and very welcome, voice came from the stairwell.

"No need for that, Doctor. I shall come to you." And

with that, the familiar figure of Sherlock Holmes began to descend the metal stairs.

"Holmes!" I cried, "Is it really—"

"Oh, Watson, don't *you* start." My old friend halted his steps when the lightkeeper brandished his harpoon. "Easy now, Otto. I merely wanted to greet my old companion." Then, to me, he asked, "What brings you here, Doctor?"

"Mrs. Hudson paid us a visit. She hadn't heard from you. She was worried."

Holmes fixed a severe expression upon George Ingalls. "It seems that my telegram to Mrs. Hudson went astray. Did you never send it?"

Ingalls, shamefaced, gave a slight shake of the head.

"My machine was down. The generator failed. It does that when the gales blow, you see—"

"And you didn't think to tell me?"

"I didn't want to disappoint you."

"Well, you *have*, Professor. Such prevarication is hardly the mark of a true Sherlockian."

I smiled to myself. So, not only was George Ingalls a Sherlockian, but he had assumed the name of Holmes's most feared criminal opponent, the late Professor Moriarty!

I couldn't help but chaff the man.

"Call yourself 'Professor Moriarty' after my stories, do you? Really, I can't imagine anyone who looks less like the dear departed Professor Moriarty—"

"That's my name in the London Society, and I suppose I've earned it!" Ingalls snapped, grabbing the packet from my hands. "I know as much about Sherlock Holmes as any man alive!"

I was about to respond when Holmes caught my

eye, shook his head disapprovingly and spoke quietly to Ingalls.

"Yes, I rather think you do, Professor. May we all go upstairs now? This basement is somewhat chilly, and it reeks of lamp-oil."

"Of course, of course."

I took a step towards the staircase, but the lightkeeper abruptly wagged his harpoon at me. As my eyes had adjusted to the light, however, I could see it was so rusted and worn that the only thing its blade might inflict was tetanus.

Still, I followed Holmes's example and asked politely if I might go upstairs.

"Yes, let the doctor go, Otto. He is our friend," Ingalls said as he checked his watch. "Meantime, I must leave for the telegraph house. The late wires will be coming in from the Continent and they'll need to be sent on to London. I shall return after Calais signs off."

"I don't suppose you could send that telegram to

Mrs. Hudson while you're at it?" Holmes asked sweetly.

"Of course! What shall I say?"

"That rather depends. Watson, do you know if Mrs. Hudson did go home for Easter?"

"No. She refused to leave London until she knew what became of you."

"Excellent. Then, pray, Ingalls, tell the good Mrs. Hudson that Dr. Watson has arrived; that I am alive and well; and by all means to go North for Easter. And sign it 'SH.'"

"I will! I will!" Ingalls appeared positively giddy at being made something of an intimate of Sherlock Holmes. He thrust the packet of sausages into the lightkeeper's hands and waved him away. "Go on, Otto, our guests will be hungry. Cook up these bangers at once!"

Then, placing his cap upon his head carefully, for the wound appeared to be quite sensitive, he exited with a disbelieving smile upon his face.

I was stuck with a deranged lightkeeper wielding a rusty old harpoon and a packet of fresh sausages.

But I had found Sherlock Holmes.

The circular staircase led us up into a large, well-lighted apartment offering spectacular views of the Downs.

Against one wall stood the fireplace, flanked by a pair of old but comfortable-looking armchairs; opposite this were a small kitchen with stove and sink, a pair of simple wooden berths, and a doorway evidently leading to the lighthouse tower. The walls of the apartment in between were covered with nautical charts marked in wax pen, and near the stairwell stood a dining table with several chairs.

And Sherlock Holmes.

"Doctor, it is so good of you to come," he said as the lightkeeper shuffled off to the kitchen with the sausages, muttering to himself.

I gripped Holmes's strong, slender hand tightly and studied my friend's face. It looked pale from lack of sleep, and an alarming tic was causing his right eye to blink rapidly.

"You haven't been injured, Holmes?"

"No, it's the lamps," he said, releasing my hand to retrieve his pipe and a thin packet of tobacco from his pocket. "Those accursed lamps."

"What lamps?"

"The lamps that make the Belle Tout light!" He nodded at the doorway. "I was given the lightkeeper's bunk room in the tower last night, through there. Could not sleep a wink. It takes thirty lamps with thirty mirrors to make the beam, you see, and the light flashes everywhere in the tower! Even into the bunk room!" He shook his head at the memory, spilling tobacco as he filled his pipe. "And that platform creaks all night!"

"What platform is this, Holmes?"

"The platform! To spin the beam!" He shook out the last of the tobacco into the bowl, spilling more as he did. Then, looking up, he apologized. "I'm sorry, Watson. You haven't been given the tour yet. The lamps are mounted on a wooden platform that spins the light beam, you see. It's turned by gears driven by giant weights hanging on chains that run straight down through the bunk room. It's like living inside an enormous grandfather clock!" His voice rose again as he tamped the tobacco into the bowl with undue violence. "*Chunk, chunk, chunk* all night long! I've not had a moment's peace in 24 hours!"

He made several attempts at striking a match and finally succeeded. Then he began inhaling long, soothing puffs, and bade me sit down at the table.

"But why are you even here, Holmes?"

"To inspect Belle Tout, and perhaps to buy it."

"Why on earth would you buy a lighthouse?"

"It's about to be decommissioned, and George Ingalls thought it might make a unique place to raise bees and conduct my chemical experiments. And the views from the lamphouse are not to be missed." He puffed sedately and shrugged his shoulders. "So, as I was coming down from London on a case…."

"That vandalism at Beachy Head?"

"Precisely. You heard about it, then?"

"Only what I read in the paper. Didn't think there was much in it for you, frankly."

"There wasn't!" Holmes blew a pensive cloud of smoke at the ceiling. "I solved it before Sir Thomas of Trinity House left my rooms at Baker Street. But I wished to confirm my deductions, so I came down that evening, took my preferred room at the Tiger, and went out yesterday morning to investigate."

He nodded at the muttering lightkeeper, now stirring a pan of hissing, snapping sausages.

"Poor Otto was up on the catwalk atop Belle Tout

and saw me picking my way down among the rocks at Beachy Head. Reckoned I was from Trinity House and had something to do with the demise of his lighthouse. Flew into an absolute rage when Ingalls brought me here after lunch. Started threatening me with his ancient harpoon—"

"But surely that old thing couldn't stop you from leaving?"

Holmes chuckled. "No, but I wanted to spend the night. Thought I might learn something."

"And did you?"

"Yes! I learned I wouldn't have made a very good lightkeeper!" He blew several precise rings of blue smoke at the ceiling. "The lights…the noise…. And it's no place to raise bees with that wind blowing off the water."

"Then I don't see the point of spending another minute here." I began to rise, but my friend shook his head and waved me back to my seat.

"I have unfinished business with the lightkeeper."

"Such as?"

He lifted an eyebrow towards the old man at the stove.

"Otto is our vandal."

"What?! The papers said it was the lads from the Eastbourne estates."

"That is what I instructed them to say."

Holmes smiled and puffed languidly on his pipe. His old assuredness was back, the tic in his eye had vanished and his voice was strong.

"It was the lightkeeper all along, as I suspected from the start. He was afraid of being made redundant. Wanted to stop the project in its tracks, and—ah, here he comes!"

The object of our conversation shuffled over and set down two plates piled high with grilled sausages.

"Excellent, Otto, thank you! Tuck in, Watson."

As the lightkeeper returned to his stove, Holmes

pushed away his plate and watched me eat.

"You traced me here by the butcher, I presume?"

I nodded.

"Yes, I thought as much," Holmes said reflectively.

"Butcher told me this was the second packet he'd sent 'round here. Couldn't imagine they were only for Otto." I spoke between mouthfuls of a rather tasty banger. "But why all these sausages, anyway?"

"It was that blasted *Naval Treaty* story of yours! 'Holmes ate his eggs and sausage with gusto,' you proclaimed to the world, and Ingalls has served me nothing but." Holmes shook his head. "With any luck, the hens will have gone on strike—"

The lightkeeper began cracking eggs into the pan.

"I spoke too soon."

"How do you stand it?"

"I don't." After a quick glance towards the kitchen, Holmes emptied his plate into one of a pair of worn rubber boots standing beneath the table. "I'm afraid whoever sticks his foot into that is going to find a rather unpleasant sensation awaits him."

"But what do you plan to do about Otto? That business at Beachy Head is rather serious. Are you going to have him arrested?"

"On the contrary, Watson. I'm going to save him." And with that curious remark, he pushed back his chair and stood up. "But first, I must replenish my pipe."

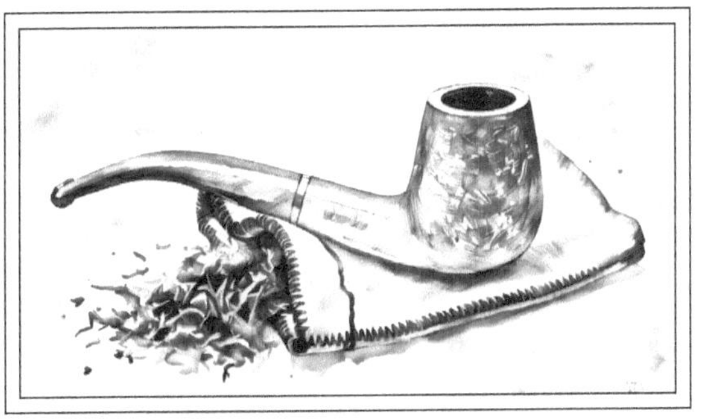

While Holmes went off in search of fresh tobacco, I took the opportunity to study the old nautical charts that covered the walls.

They had been marked, as I say, with wax pencil notations of water depth, tides, shoals, and shipwrecks by the various Belle Tout lightkeepers over the years.

Next to the fireplace, however, there stood a telltale square of wood paneling not yellowed by time, where one of the charts had evidently been removed and the blank space filled with fresh writing—not in wax pencil but in black pen.

I counted a dozen lines of varying lengths, all written in a feverish, intense hand, the words interrupted in many places by arrows, dashes, insertions, exclamation points, and question marks.

Many question marks.

I was wondering what to make of it when Sherlock Holmes—his tobacco quest unsuccessful—joined me, an inscrutable smile upon his face.

"What is this?" I asked.

"Can't you tell?"

Looking closer, it took some few moments to realize that the twelve lines of writing contained occurrences from a life.

And not just any life.

It was the life of Sherlock Holmes.

I was staggered.

"Who did this?"

"George Ingalls. He wrote it all out last night while I was trying to sleep."

"He's made a timeline of your life!"

Holmes waved his unlit pipe at the text. "The George

Ingalls version of it, anyway."

"Yes, it is quite fanciful. Where did he get all these… ideas from?"

"The same place he divined that I eat nothing but eggs and sausages, Watson! Your stories."

"But this is all wrong. I never wrote *this*!" I tapped the first entry. "'Born January 6th, on a country estate in North Riding—'"

"No, you certainly didn't."

"'—to parents named Siger and Violet Holmes?' This is utter madness!"

My friend chuckled and shook his head.

"It's not quite so mad as one might think, Doctor. I've had some time to ponder that entry. Do you recall your story of *The Empty House*, when I told you of my time in Tibet meeting the Dalai Lama?"

"Yes, of course."

"And I said I traveled there in disguise, as a Norwegian explorer named Sigerson? Well, 'Sigerson' could mean '*Siger's son*,' could it not? Therefore, my father would have been named 'Siger.'"

"I suppose," I said doubtfully. "But why, then, 'Violet' for your mother?"

"Because you bestowed that name upon at least three women in your stories, Watson. No doubt Ingalls reasoned it was a clue to my mother's true name."

"If you say so, Holmes. But what about this idea here—that you have an 'Older brother named Sherrinford.' Does such a person even exist?"

"Of course not. There is only Mycroft and me. But that, too, is quite clever. Perhaps his most clever deduction of all—"

"I'd like to know how!"

"Simplicity itself: The existence of an older brother would explain why neither Mycroft nor I inherited that so-called country estate in North Riding. Such an estate would have gone to our elder brother, would it not?"

"Well, yes. But why would he think you were born January 6th?"

"I haven't a clue, Watson. Not a clue."

"Of course, you never told me your true birthday, Holmes. Or much of anything else, for that matter. You only ever said you were descended from 'country squires.'"

"Indeed, I did say that," he answered, a wry smile upon his face.

"There *were* country squires in your family, were there not?"

Holmes's smile became a noiseless chuckle.

"You mean that was all a lie?" I asked sharply.

"More of a ruse, I should think."

I fairly lost my temper at this.

"Ruse or lie, Holmes, it's the same thing. I passed that 'ruse' onto my readers, you know! And they trust me!" I pointed at the 'country estate' entry on the wall. "See there? George Ingalls believed it, thanks to me!"

"Yes, and a good thing he did."

"What do you mean?"

"I wanted readers like Ingalls to believe it. I wanted *all* your readers to believe it. And how could they believe it unless *you* did, too?"

"So, you deliberately lied to me—"

"I wasn't lying to *you*, Watson. I was lying to my enemies." He clapped a hand upon my shoulder and looked into my eyes. "Did it never occur to you, Doctor, that those stories of yours were read not only by my admirers, but by men who wanted to do away with me?"

I couldn't bring myself to speak. I was ashamed to admit such a thought had never crossed my mind.

"In fact, Mycroft and I were orphans, as you had always suspected. But we didn't want the truth so broadly known."

"I'm sorry, Holmes. I don't know what to say...."

"Then say nothing, take a seat and listen."

He guided me into one of the armchairs before the fireplace, where last night's embers lay cooling in the grate, and took a seat in the other.

"Brother Mycroft never liked the idea of you writing up our cases," he began. "There had been so many adversaries bent upon my destruction over the years that he thought it could only lead to a bad end for me. But I pointed out that your first few stories had brought clients of enormous benefit to the crown, so he relented—on the condition that I alter the facts a bit."

"Then you made up that red herring about the country squires?"

"*Mycroft* made it up. I merely worked it into a conversation with you when the opportunity arose."

"But why let me write up our cases at all, if it was putting you in danger?"

Holmes sighed and shook his head.

"Vanity, Watson. The truth is, I enjoyed being celebrated. Pains me to say so, but there it is. And of course, that fame brought me some of the most abstruse and absorbing cases any man could claim."

"They also brought you obsessives like George Ingalls," I said ruefully. "I imagine you overheard his interrogation of me when I first arrived?"

Holmes nodded. "But I rather think that was the bump on his head talking, not a madman. You really ought to look at that injury when he returns."

"What of his timeline, then?" I stood up and paced before the wall. "Don't you think this is going too far? Fake estates, fake parents, fake brothers—"

"And fake marriages!" Holmes rose and pointed to a later entry. "Did you know you've been married three times?"

"*What*?"

"Says so right here: '3rd wife hinted at in *The Illustrious Client*....'"

"Why, he's made me out to be some kind of randy Casanova with a doctor's kit!"

"Don't be upset, Watson. If you can be married three times, I can have a relation who was 'close to' Jack the Ripper. See here?"

Sure enough, a long entry speculated on exactly that, with dates, names, arrows, and exclamation points.

I threw up my hands. "This is delusional, Holmes. You must put an end to it."

"On the contrary, Watson, this is exactly what Mycroft would have hoped to see: false trails everywhere to keep my enemies at bay! Besides," he shrugged, "I don't see that it brings harm to anyone—"

"It harms *me*," I said hotly. "Three marriages? What if that idea got around? How would I explain it to Margaret? To my patients?"

"*Pshaw*, Doctor! This hasn't exactly been written on the front page of the *Times*, has it? We stand before the wall of a lighthouse soon to be decommissioned, and one day to fall into the sea."

"But I brought your methods to the public so they

might do some good, not to set off lurid speculation that mocks me and you and all your achievements. Come now, Jack the *Ripper*? What if Scotland Yard got wind of that? Or the *Times*? That could be very embarrassing to your brother Mycroft, could it not?"

Holmes's brow furrowed, and he looked closer at the writing.

"Yes, Watson, I suppose you're right—"

There was a sudden clatter from the kitchen where the lightkeeper was sliding a huge pan of scrambled eggs onto a platter.

"But I see the eggs are ready, and we must return to the vicinity of those rubber boots before they are served."

He patted me on the shoulder as we walked.

"I'll have a little chat with George Ingalls about all this before we leave."

"I should hope so. It must stop."

"It will, Watson. It will."

OTTO SET THE GIANT PLATE of eggs on the table before us, but instead of turning back to the kitchen, he stood twisting his wool cap anxiously in his hands.

"What is it?" Holmes asked in a kindly voice.

"Half hour 'til sunset. Time to light the lamps. But I can't do it alone."

"Oh?"

"Aye. Takes two men, you see. The Professor usually helps, but he ain't here, so…."

Holmes shot a glance my way, then smiled at the lightkeeper.

"Tell me Otto. Would *three* men suffice?"

"Oh, more than suffice!"

"Well, Watson, what do you say?"

"I say we help light the lamps!"

"How about it, Otto?

"I thank ye both!"

The old man placed his cap upon his head and waved us to follow him to the doorway.

"Thank goodness," murmured Holmes as we entered the tower, leaving the eggs behind. "That boot was almost full."

THE LIGHTKEEPER'S REPRIEVE

The winding stone staircase took us up into the lamphouse at the very top of the tower.

It was a large, octagonal, glass-enclosed room smelling strongly of paraffin, and in the center stood the heart of Belle Tout: a giant tubular brass structure, looking not unlike an enormous, three-sided metal Christmas tree, with thirty lamps arrayed around it, ten lamps per side. Each lamp was backed by a highly polished mirror to reflect its light, and each was fed lamp-oil through the brass tubing of the "tree" from a giant cask of paraffin one level below us.

The entire "tree" stood on a round wooden platform that could be set in motion by the release of two giant weights suspended on massive chains that dropped slowly through holes in the lamp-house floor, turning gears to spin the platform, causing the three-sided light beam to shine out of the lamphouse windows and sweep across the waters of the English Channel and the rolling hills of the South Downs, one full rotation every two minutes.

But first, those lamps had to be lit.

And now Otto came alive before our eyes.

Gone was the muttering lightkeeper with the quivering, rusted harpoon. In his place was a vigorous taskmaster who knew what was required of us and never hesitated to make certain we got it right.

After handing us long, thin tapers, he demonstrated how to light the lamps just so, making certain no wax dripped onto the reflective mirrors. Then, when we had proven we could manage that task to his satisfaction, he set to work performing the intricate business of adjusting the mirrors behind each lamp so their accumulated light could be focused into a most powerful, and surprisingly hot, three-part beam.

Half an hour later, when the lamps were all lit and the beam its brightest, Otto released a metal lever beside the platform that set the two giant weights on their slow descent, causing the platform to creak to life beneath our feet.

Then he motioned us to follow him out of the lamphouse onto the catwalk, where he could judge how the light beam was performing.

Stepping outside onto an iron grate one hundred feet above the ground, and perhaps two hundred or more feet above the waters of the English Channel, Holmes and I found ourselves occupying the best viewing platform in the South Downs, with unimpeded views in every direction—so long as one could maintain a grip on the iron railings, for the biting wind blew so fiercely it seemed to be trying to lift the entire structure and send it crashing into the sea!

But Otto paid no attention to this forceful reminder

of nature's might.

He was studying man's own creation—the Belle Tout beam—as it swept across the waters far out to sea. And by the proud look upon his face, he was satisfied.

"Tell me, Otto," Holmes shouted against the wind as the lightkeeper eyed the beam piercing the gathering gloom. "How far does that shine?"

"23 miles! See there?" The lightkeeper pointed to a freighter suddenly illuminated by the light from Belle Tout. "That there's the *Cantlemere*. She's 20 miles out, bound for Rotterdam."

"Remarkable!"

"Just wait, though!" Otto's eyes stayed fixed as the beam swept past the *Cantlemere* and she was lost in darkness.

We waited for what seemed like several minutes. Then, the long, deep blast of a ship's horn swept over us like a sustained rumble of thunder.

"That's her!" Otto exclaimed. "The captain always

thanks me as she passes!"

He touched his forehead in tribute, and I saw in his eyes a gleam I shall never forget, evincing pride and satisfaction for a job well done.

But his pleased countenance did not last long.

And I regret to say I was the cause of its dissipation.

Out of the corner of my eye, I had noticed—perhaps a mile to the east along the beach—the shadowy form of a half-built tower, which I surmised could only be the new lighthouse going up at Beachy Head.

And I recalled something I had read in the newspaper story about it.

"Tell me," I said to Otto, "I understand the reason for the new lighthouse is the way the fog pushes up the cliffs here, it obscures the beam. Is that true?"

It was a question I instantly regretted.

"You tellin' me they get no fog at Beachy Head?" Otto pointed an accusatory finger into my chest. "You sayin' somethin' stops it from blowin' there too?"

"Well, they say the fog comes over the cliffs a certain way here—"

"*They* say? They say? Who says?"

"I read it in the paper—"

But Sherlock Holmes cut me off with a shake of his head, and I fell silent while the lightkeeper sputtered his objections.

"Read it in the paper… he read it in the paper…."

At that moment, the construction at Beachy Head was lit up by the Belle Tout beam. Tendrils of fog could be seen creeping over the large granite blocks and circling the carpenter's shed where the vandalism had taken place.

The lightkeeper came alive. "See, there? See it? Ain't that the same fog as Belle Tout?"

"Indeed, it is, Otto," Holmes said quietly. "The very same."

A smile crept to Otto's lips, and he nodded.

"Tha's right, Mr. Holmes. Tha's exackly right."

I knew—as did Holmes, I was sure—that it wasn't "'exackly' right."

The erosion of the cliffs below Belle Tout made her vulnerable to fog in a way its builders had not foreseen, and the Beachy Head light was being constructed on

the beach itself, where the fog would pass beneath the light.

But by the glare from my companion, I dared not

argue the point.

"I'm sorry," I said instead. "It's been some years since I've experienced fog like this. Not since my return from Afghanistan—"

"Oh, eh?" Otto's mutterings ceased. "What regiment?"

"66th Berkshire. Battle of Maiwand. And you served…where?"

"HMS *Cordelia*, sir. Under Hume, that was."

"Ah! The New Zealand wars. You had a rough journey home, I know."

"Aye, that we did." Otto turned his eyes upon a second freighter now exposed by the light beam as she cut through the waters far offshore. "Typhoon come up before we could blink. But we all pulled together and made it through. That we did. Not like today, when nobody pulls together…."

He fell silent, as did we all.

A few moments later, however, Sherlock Holmes

tapped my arm and winked. Then he cleared his throat and began speaking in a conversational tone loud enough to be overheard by the lightkeeper.

"I say, Watson, did that newspaper story say anything about what the vandals got up to at Beachy Head?"

"Why, yes, Holmes," said I, catching something of my friend's intent by the glint in his eye. "Lamp-oil dumped on the blocks so they couldn't be lifted into place, as I recall. And a dead jellyfish left in the carpenter's hut."

"Yes, and a very poisonous species, too! A bad business, it was."

"Still, the police put it down to some toughs from the Eastbourne estates," I said with a shrug.

"They did, Watson, they did. But Sir Thomas of Trinity House wasn't satisfied. He thought there must be more to it. Asked me to have a look. I spent yesterday morning combing those rocks, looking for clues."

The lightkeeper stiffened.

"And did you find any?" I asked.

"I did. An empty cask of lamp-oil was dashed on the rocks. And do you know, it looked very much like those casks in the basement here."

The lightkeeper began muttering, and his hands seemed to be groping for the harpoon he had left behind.

"Indeed, Holmes!"

"Yes, and did you happen to notice the fishing rod by the door when you came in?"

"What of it?"

"There's a piece of squid still baited to the hook. And I'm told the jellyfish in these waters do enjoy their squid."

The lightkeeper was now shaking, his mutterings intense.

"What do you make of it, Holmes? What are you going to tell Sir Thomas?"

The lightkeeper had stopped breathing, and I thought he might faint.

I braced myself to support him.

"I'm going to tell Sir Thomas," Holmes said, placing a gentle hand on the shoulder of the trembling figure in the wool cap, "the lads from the estate pinched a cask of oil and that fishing rod from Belle Tout and ran riot at the new lighthouse."

Otto let out such a long, sighing breath I thought he might faint from relief!

"And that's the end of it?"

"Not entirely. Tomorrow morning I'll be dropping a line to Trinity House telling Sir Thomas the only acceptable payment for my services will be the appointment of our friend Otto here as the locum for the new lightkeeper at Beachy Head. That is, if Otto agrees."

Holmes looked questioningly at the lightkeeper, who stared at him open-mouthed.

"But do you think Sir Thomas will agree, Holmes?"

"I can assure you, Doctor, he'll have no choice."

With that, Otto hugged my friend.

And began to cry.

Deerstalkers on the Downs

We left the much-relieved lightkeeper to his scrutiny of the Channel waters and circled the catwalk to the landward side. The Downs now spread out before us like a three-dimensional map enshrouded in the gathering darkness, the scattered farmhouses and cottages of East Dean discernable only by the flickering of yellow lamps in their windows.

"That was very kind of you back there," I said after a time. "And a very wise solution, I might add."

My friend dismissed the compliment—as he had always dismissed such encomiums—with a wave of his hand.

"You can't replace thirty years' knowledge of those

waters with just anybody. Sir Thomas would have learned that soon enough—" Holmes abruptly stopped speaking.

Something had caught his eye.

Then I saw it too: several flickering lights from the vicinity of East Dean appeared to be moving. Out onto the Downs. Towards us.

"What do you make of it, Holmes?"

"I can't say."

"Searching for a lost dog, perhaps?"

The several lights multiplied into half a dozen distinct lights.

"That would be a very large search party for a lost dog, Watson."

The number doubled again.

"Sheep, then?"

Holmes scratched his chin. "That's no search party, Watson...."

"What is it?"

He chuckled and shook his head as the movement quickened.

"It's Ingalls. George Ingalls. He's bringing them all here."

"Bringing all who here?"

"The Sherlockians, Watson." He smiled grimly. "The blasted Sherlockians."

"All the way from London?"

"All the way from London."

"I don't believe it."

At that moment, the Belle Tout light swept across the Downs, lighting up the moving figures like the noonday sun. They could be seen holding torches and wearing capes, and upon their heads, deerstalker hats. I counted twelve in all.

"Do you believe it now, Watson?"

FOR HALF AN HOUR WE watched them that way, their progress exposed in brief flashes each time the beam caught them: bunched together waiting to pass through a turnstile; marching single file across a pasture; climbing over a gate; crossing the next pasture.

With George Ingalls always in the lead.

When they reached the cliff walk for the final dash up the bluff to Belle Tout, Holmes signaled it was time for us to go inside. We bade Otto good-night, entered the lamphouse, and began making our way down the tower staircase as the excited voices of a dozen Sherlockians suddenly rose up from the living quarters to meet our ears.

"Why have they come here, Holmes?"

"To discuss my life, I suppose. And fill in all those question marks on that wall."

"You're going to have to tell them the truth, then. You must set them straight, you know."

"Yes," he said, with a sigh. "I suppose I must."

"Enough is enough."

"Leave it to me, Watson. Leave it to me."

And with that, we entered the apartment, where the ecstatic figure of George Ingalls greeted Holmes.

"They all came!" he cried. "Every member of the London Society came!"

"Yes," said my friend with no little asperity. "It seems they did."

Ingalls looked crestfallen. "I thought you would be honored."

"Did you at least send the telegram to Mrs. Hudson?"

"Of course!" Ingalls handed over a confirmation receipt from the District Office in London. Holmes glanced at the paper and stuffed it in his pocket.

"Very well, then. Lead on."

A Confession is Made

It had come to this: Sherlock Holmes facing a crowd of his most ardent admirers, prepared to refute the life story created by those same admirers—a life story written out on the wall behind him like a biblical canon.

They were middle-aged men for the most part, although one or two younger faces peered out beneath the caps, and three were women, hair piled up beneath their deerstalkers.

In place of the torches that had shown them the way across the Downs, they now held pencils and either a book—one of my books—or a dog-eared edition of one of the magazines in which the stories had been serialized.

They had come prepared to take notes of everything their *beau idéal* said.

Quite naturally, the presence of so many people crammed together had caused the living quarters to warm up considerably, and the heavy scent of old sausages and scrambled eggs only added to the stuffy atmosphere.

But it did nothing to dampen the excitement and expectations of these men and women, and I thought it best to remove myself from the crowd, taking a seat at the table after pushing away the plate of eggs that had long grown cold.

As I studied the earnest faces before me, I couldn't help but dread the outcome.

How would they react when Sherlock Holmes demolished their fantastical 'biography' of his life?

Would they be appreciative of his honesty?

Or would they turn against him, as the poor lightkeeper had done when he thought my friend had come to shut down Belle Tout; and as George Ingalls had turned against *me* when I tried to explain my stories?

I recalled the man's sudden outbursts—the anger and the popping eyes—and I began to consider how we might extricate ourselves from that confined space if things went wrong. The wooden dining table, I decided, could serve as a barricade to help keep an escape route open to the staircase, if need be. As for a weapon—if for some reason it came to that—I briefly considered the rubber boot at my feet.

Being full of old sausages, I guessed it might be heavy enough to serve as a kind of truncheon. But it wouldn't *look* like a weapon, and I only wanted something that might cause an angry crowd to have second thoughts about pursuit.

Then, I remembered just the thing.

And while all eyes were on Sherlock Holmes, I made my way to the kitchen as if to fetch a glass of water, then

I grabbed the item in mind, returned to my seat at the table and rested the artifact across my knees, making it easy to grasp but hidden from view.

It was the lightkeeper's ridiculous harpoon.

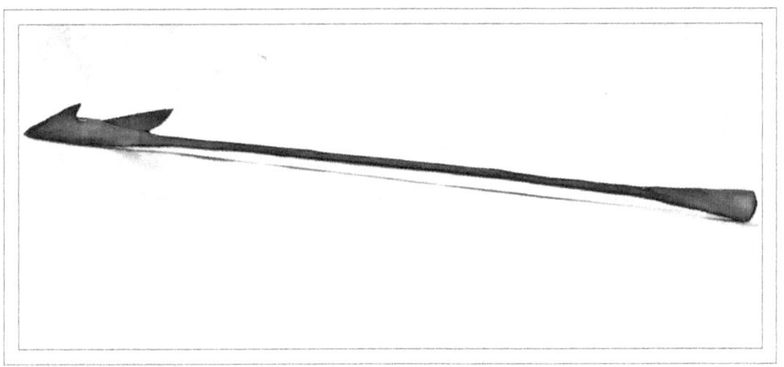

The encounter got underway.

Ingalls, speaking as 'Professor Moriarty,' introduced each member of the London Society by their chosen sobriquet.

They included 'Wiggins' of the Baker Street Irregulars, Holmes's brother 'Mycroft,' Scotland Yard's 'Inspector Lestrade,' the villainous 'John Clay' and 'Jonathan Small'—even 'Arthur Charpentier' and

'Major Sholto' among the men, and of course, Holmes's favorite of women: 'Irene Adler.'

Then, he gave the floor to Sherlock Holmes himself, to say a few words before the questioning would begin.

"Thank you, Professor."

I took in my breath as Holmes paused and surveyed the expectant assembly with hard, grey eyes, for I knew what disdain that somber countenance could hold.

The crowd seemed to sense it, too.

The smiles beneath the deerstalkers weakened and then vanished, replaced by more quizzical expressions. As Holmes's pause lengthened, there was a holding of breath, and soon the only sound to be heard was the low rumble of the wooden platform in the tower, and the chunk, chunk, chunk of the metal weights descending slowly through the bunk room.

Finally, my friend began.

"First, I have a confession to make."

A kind of alertness took hold of the deerstalkers.

Their postures changed. There was a tilting of heads and craning of ears as they waited to hear what followed this ominous-sounding opening, until the silence was broken not by Sherlock Holmes, but by the sharp smack of a book hitting the floor, followed by a scuffling.

It was George Ingalls.

His apprehension at what Holmes might say had caused his copy of *Hound of the Baskervilles* to slip out of his trembling hands, and his clumsy attempts to pick it up were unsuccessful. The poor man's shoulders were shaking uncontrollably, and he appeared to be crying. 'Irene Adler' separated herself from the crowd and moved to Ingalls's side, retrieving the book and putting her arm around the man before raising her face to Sherlock Holmes and glaring in such a way that my old friend was considerably startled, and his expression softened.

Then his eyes lost their ominous portent and took

on an appearance of empathy.

A new determination seemed to come to Sherlock Holmes.

He glanced at me with a questioning look, which, after the countless nights and days we had spent together in every imaginable circumstance—tracking phosphorescent hounds, evil stepfathers, and master jewel thieves—I could read from across the room.

I nodded my assent, and Holmes cleared his throat before resuming his address to the deerstalkers.

"The confession I must make, Professor," he said in a now-kindly voice, "is simply this: I don't enjoy sausage and eggs quite as much as you think I do. And let me show you where I've been hiding the evidence!"

He waved in my direction.

"Dr. Watson, would you do the honors?"

A curious murmuring arose as all eyes turned on me.

I set the old harpoon on the floor and picked up the

rubber boot. Then I held it over the table and turned it upside down. A gelatinous mass of uneaten sausages began oozing out onto the plate of cold eggs.

A gasp went up from the crowd, then murmurs of surprise and wonder.

"I'm afraid Dr. Watson misled his readers with that little tale of *The Naval Treaty*," Holmes said above the murmuring. Then, in a conspiratorial fashion, he added, "On occasion, I do enjoy a good steak. Isn't that right, Doctor?"

"Yes," said I, leaving the boot behind and making my way through the astonished crowd to join my old friend. "We both do!"

As I passed 'Irene Adler,' I could see she was now smiling at Sherlock Holmes—she had a most wonderful smile—and that Holmes was returning it with his own. Then, to the Sherlockian who called himself 'Inspector Lestrade,' Holmes said, "I hope you won't arrest me for hiding the evidence, Inspector!"

'Lestrade' shook his head and burst out laughing, and soon we were all laughing together.

Even George Ingalls.

Rolling Away the Stone

Their questions had come at Sherlock Holmes for three straight hours, and he had answered them all in his most precise and didactic manner…and entirely in accordance with the timeline on the wall.

All the questions but one.

When it came to his true birth year, Holmes had changed the subject—to his pipe. Or more particularly, to his lack of pipe tobacco.

"Before I answer that most excellent question about the true year of my birth, does anyone have spare tobacco I might partake of?" he had asked, displaying the empty pipe.

There was a scramble as coat pockets were searched.

Finally, a pouch was offered, its owner saying proudly,

"It's shag tobacco, of course!"

"My favorite! How did you know?"

"*A Scandal in Bohemia!*" a half-dozen Sherlockians cried out in unison.

"Only *A Scandal in Bohemia*?" Holmes asked with mock surprise.

"*Silver Blaze!*" another Sherlockian spoke up.

"Excellent!" said Holmes.

"And *Twisted Lip!*" added another.

"Bravo!"

"Don't forget *Hound of the Baskervilles!*" said George Ingalls, waving his copy, and Sherlock Holmes shook his head in mock disapprobation.

"How could anyone forget *Baskerville*, Professor? I think it's the doctor's finest work yet, wouldn't you agree?"

Ingalls nodded vigorously and there was applause in some quarters, but disagreement elsewhere. Soon a hotly contested debate was raging among the Sherlockians about their favorite story, while Holmes and I looked on, smiling to one another.

They failed to see it, of course: Sherlock Holmes had caused them to entirely forget the question of his true birth year.

All but 'Irene Adler,' who gazed at Sherlock Holmes with a look of no little admiration upon her face.

IT WAS NEAR MIDNIGHT WHEN Holmes and I stepped outside into a wind that felt even colder and sharper than on the catwalk atop Belle Tout. My companion took his time buttoning his coat and readying his walking stick for the journey back to the Tiger.

He was waiting for the lighthouse beam to sweep the countryside before us.

When it finally did, he glanced up at the tower and gave a wave to Otto, who saluted back from the catwalk.

"I don't know how you managed it, Holmes," I said as we stepped out onto the footpath. "You made that timeline come alive! Every supposition, from country squires to the mythical estate in North Riding, to that so-called third brother of yours!"

"And don't forget my relations with Jack the Ripper," Holmes added with a chuckle.

"Yes. I'm only sorry you felt compelled to confirm a third marriage for me."

"Needs must, Doctor. I had to give them what they wanted."

"God knows what Margaret will say. Still, the way you avoided giving up your birth year was cleverly done."

"Well, I thought you might like to work that into one of your stories someday." He smiled. "You'll leave it vague, of course."

"Of course. I always have."

We walked on, lost in our own thoughts, the light of a waxing moon showing the way. As the chalky footpath took us closer to the lights of East Dean, however, I broke the silence.

"Still, I didn't much like seeing that question-mark at the end of the timeline: *'SH dies, 19__?'* It made me shiver."

"Nonsense, Watson. One day, George Ingalls or somebody like him will fill in that date, and life will go on. Ashes to ashes, you know."

"Is that what this retirement business is all about? Is there something about your health you haven't told me?"

"Not a bit. I feel as healthy as the day we met at Bart's. And that's rather the point: to retire from the detective field while I can, not when I must."

"Well, I have my doubts. I've tried to leave the medical profession behind more than once, you know, but I find nothing can replace the mental stimulation."

"Oh, I have no apprehension about finding stimulation here, Watson. There will be beekeeping to master, and my chemical experiments…. And just look at those stars, and that moon. How bright it shines! How close it appears!"

At that moment, however, the great yellow beam of Belle Tout caught us in its brilliance, blinding us to the moon and the stars in the sky.

Holmes shielded his eyes and chuckled. "And, of course, Otto's light reminds us that there is beauty in our own creations, too."

I slept late next morning, Saturday, and spent the rest of the day arranging my wife's journey to East Dean to celebrate Easter with Sherlock Holmes and me.

Holmes spent the day visiting properties with George Ingalls, and I didn't see him until Sunday morning, when I was alone having breakfast at the Tiger and he burst in from his walk.

"Get your coat, Watson. I've found it!"

"Found what?"

But he was already out the door and I didn't catch up until he had reached the far side of the green. From there, we followed the cobblestones of Went Way to

the very last house—the empty cottage of the widow Dunbar.

Holmes turned to me. "Well, what do you think?"

"That old pile?"

"That old pile." His eyes glittered as he surveyed the sad-looking house so badly in need of repair.

"Surely you don't mean it?"

"Oh, but I do. Ingalls is bringing the papers to the Tiger after church. Come, let me show you."

But we did not go inside.

It was the overgrown orchard out back that most appealed to Holmes.

He gazed approvingly at the apple trees which, though untended and badly pruned, were alive with bees crawling inside the thick white petals. He waved at the many white puffs of thistle floating lazily in the air before us, released on their journey by an industrious goldfinch in the hedge. And he laughed with delight when a small black snake suddenly propelled itself across the stone flagging before vanishing into the overgrowth, causing me to jump.

"There!" he said, grabbing my arm as the sun crept above the tiny figure of Belle Tout a mile distant. "You see how the sun moves across the sky here? With these apple trees and that life-giving light, I think we will fashion a most excellent apiary."

He gestured towards the lighthouse.

"And that proud tower on the horizon will forever remind me of 'The Good Friday Encounter.'"

"The Good Friday *what?*"

"My encounter with those Sherlockians on Friday evening. Ingalls added it to his timeline. It is a part of their history, now."

"Goodness, Holmes. You really have given into their monomania!"

"No, Doctor. I've bequeathed them something of my life, that is all."

"But it's still *your* life, Holmes."

"Not anymore, Watson. Not anymore."

He lapsed into silence as he studied the industrious bees toiling close at hand. Then his eyes shifted to the newly foaled lambs in the sheep pen just beyond the stone wall, while far away gulls soared on drafts above distant chalk cliffs, and, well out to sea, unseen freighters plowed through the roiling waters.

Suddenly, the bells of the parish church came to our ears. Holmes, stirring from his revery, placed a gentle hand upon my shoulder.

"It's time, old friend. The church bell tolls…and it tolls for thee and me. Our London guests will be arriving at the Tiger any minute."

It was only then that I remembered it was Easter Sunday.

The Detective and the Dalai Lama

The pews in the sanctuary of the church of St. Simon and St. Jude overflowed with the country folk of East Dean, and not a few Londoners.

There were Holmes and myself, of course; Mrs. Watson (my *second* wife, not my third—whatever the Sherlockians may say!), Holmes's brother Mycroft and our old friend Inspector Lestrade.

There was, too, the loyal Mrs. Hudson, who had decided to join her missing lodger for Easter rather than visit her family in the North as planned.

"I thought it might be the last Easter I ever spent with Mr. Holmes," she had said as I helped her out of the cab from Eastbourne.

There were also, I might add, the Sherlockians.

All twelve, led by George Ingalls.

His forehead cleaned and bandaged—I had put my medical kit to use before leaving Belle Tout with Holmes after the 'Good Friday Encounter'—Ingalls and the others had spent the previous two nights at the lighthouse and seemed to have been entirely unfazed by the lights and noise that had so disturbed Sherlock Holmes.

As Ingalls explained, "We talked of nothing but the Encounter! We never noticed the lights or the noise!"

THE VICAR'S EASTER HOMILY WAS a good one, its theme being that we should all be prepared to "Roll Away the Stone" at times in our lives, and the closing hymn was a rousing *Eternal Father, Strong to Save*, one of Sherlock Holmes's favorites.

After the service we all made our way across the green to the Tiger—Sherlockians too— and shared an excellent French Beaune while Sherlock Holmes sat in the snug with George Ingalls and signed the papers necessary to purchase the Dunbar cottage.

Then we all sat down at a row of tables to enjoy a hearty Easter meal prepared by Jack the landlord, who grilled the lambs, and Grace, his wife, who made the pies.

George Ingalls sat at our table, with the stipulation (insisted upon by brother Mycroft) that should he so much as *breathe* a question of Sherlock Holmes that might tread upon affairs of state, Ingalls and his Sherlockians would be drummed out of the Tiger.

But Mycroft needn't have worried.

So awestruck was Ingalls in the company of individuals about whom he had only read in books and magazines that he spent most of the meal shifting his gaze from that of Mycroft Holmes talking with Sherlock in a kind of brotherly shorthand about all manner of subjects, to Mrs. Hudson and Inspector Lestrade, who (to his evident surprise) got on quite famously.

As the meal progressed and the wine flowed, however, Ingalls grew more relaxed, and when the discussion between Mycroft and Sherlock turned from the Christian Easter story to Tibetan Buddhist views of life and the afterlife, Ingalls could restrain himself no more.

"'The Great Hiatus!'" he blurted out, causing all heads to turn.

"What was that?" Mycroft asked, thoroughly confused.

"The years Dr. Watson thought your brother was dead, but it turned out he was in disguise, travelling in Tibet. We call that 'The Great Hiatus!'"

"There was nothing 'great' about it," said Mrs. Hudson sharply. "We were shattered. Weren't we,

Doctor?"

I nodded, but George Ingalls had turned his ever-enthusiastic face to Sherlock Holmes.

"Did you *really* meet the head lama in Lhasa? What did you discuss? Can he really fly through the air like a bird, as they say he can?"

Sherlock looked to Mycroft, who could only smile and shake his head in wonder at the boundless enthusiasm of the dedicated Sherlockians.

Finally, with a wink at his brother, Mycroft capitulated.

"Why don't we just 'roll away the stone' on your time in Tibet, Sherlock. Go on. Tell them what happened when you met the Dalai Lama."

And Sherlock Holmes did.

EPILOGUE

Gazing south towards the English Channel from a tidy apple orchard near the village of East Dean, one can see in the distance the figure of a lighthouse that once kept watch, as the old hymn says, "for those in peril on the sea."

Long since decommissioned—the barrels of paraffin that fed its lamps removed; the lamps themselves dismantled and given away; the heavy clocklike mechanism that turned the platform melted down for guns during the Great War—Belle Tout is now a holiday let that offers unmatched views of the English Channel to the south and the Sussex Downs to the north.

But the views from its tower are not her only attraction.

Upon a patch of wall beside the fireplace in the living quarters there appear a dozen lines of text, written in black ink by a feverish hand, that purport to tell the life story of a man: a man whose adventurous career brought him fame across several continents—at a time when continents were connected only by sailing ships and the telegraph wire—thanks to the stories written by a loyal friend who had participated in more than a few adventures with that good man.

Many who book a stay at Belle Tout do so mainly to study those twelve long lines of writing on the wall in detail, while others do it for the views from the tower and for the bracing walks the local footpaths ensure.

In either case, should residents of Belle Tout follow the footpath across the Downs to the village of East Dean, they will pass the small, tidy apple orchard mentioned above. They may even see a slender, elderly gentleman keeping watch upon the beehives and the apple trees there and they may mistake him for a gardener.

But if they were to take the time to stop and watch the man go about his work, they might discern

something in the keenly perceptive manner with which he studies his winged charges that calls to mind the man described in those lines scribbled upon the wall at Belle Tout—a man who once made his living by helping others through the systematic observation of human behavior.

And if they could bring themselves to interrupt that diligent and determined beekeeper to ask if he was indeed the same person as the man described on that wall, he will, it has been reported, look past the hives and the apple trees and the greening pastures with their white sheep to the distant figure of Belle Tout, and gently shake his head.

"No, not anymore," he will say.

Then he will smile and politely excuse himself and return to the garden.

And his bees.

The End

ACKNOWLEDGEMENTS

This book owes its existence to editor David Marcum, graphic artist David Greenberg and reader June Miller.

David Marcum is the superlative editor of MX Publishing's "New Sherlock Holmes" anthologies and his call for a submission to what would be the last in his long series prompted me to think about a request from June Miller a couple of years before.

June is a loyal reader from just outside Glasgow, in Scotland, and I love hearing from her. One day, after reading the Christmas story I called *The Case of the Disappearing Beaune*, June asked if I had ever thought about writing a Sherlock Holmes Easter story.

I hadn't, but in that moment, I knew I'd have to—it was too good an idea.

And yet, the story came slowly. Not until David Marcum's last call for submissions did the idea of Sherlock getting kidnapped—in a fashion—by a band of earnest Sherlockians come to mind.

After that, the story came quickly: Sherlock, pondering retirement, decides to leave behind his old life for these Sherlockian "disciples" to interpret, while he moves on to a new life tending his bees in the South Downs.

A real Easter story.

But then came the hard part: producing this slender, beautiful volume. For that, the keen eyes and diligent hard work of David Greenberg, whose superlative artistic skills I have known since grade school, made it happen.

Hence, the novella you hold in your hands.

~ J. L. Matthews

J. Lawrence Matthews has contributed fiction to the *New York Times* and NPR's *All Things Considered* and is the author of *One Must Tell the Bees: Abraham Lincoln and the Final Education of Sherlock Holmes* (East Dean Press, 2021).

Called "beautifully written and immediately engaging" in The Sherlock Holmes Society of London summer journal, *One Must Tell the Bees* remains the first and only novel to bring Sherlock Holmes together with Abraham Lincoln during the American Civil War.

Previously, during a long career on Wall Street, Matthews wrote *Pilgrimage to Warren Buffett's Omaha* (McGraw-Hill, 2010) and authored a financial blog called, appropriately, *Jeff Matthews is Not Making This Up*.

He is currently at work on the sequel to *One Must Tell the Bees*, which will take Sherlock Holmes to Tibet in 1891 for an encounter with the 13th Dalai Lama that foreshadows the current predicament of his reincarnation, the 14th Dala Lama, with respect to the Communist Chinese Government's naked attempt to take control of Tibetan Buddhism.

Matthews resides in Naples, FL with his wife Nancy, where his favorite breaks from writing are book club meetings in person (or virtually) with his readers, visits from children and grandchildren, and, when the house gets a little too quiet, playing the drums. Loud.

www.ingramcontent.com/pod-product-compliance
Lightning Source LLC
Chambersburg PA
CBHW061456210726
48287CB00007B/2532